Ultimate Science Lab

NOISY EXPERIMENTS

Anna Claybourne

Gareth Stevens
PUBLISHING

Please visit our website, www.garethstevens.com. For a free color catalog of all our high-quality books, call toll free 1-800-542-2595 or fax 1-877-542-2596.

Cataloging-in-Publication Data

Names: Claybourne, Anna.
Title: Noisy experiments / Anna Claybourne.
Description: New York : Gareth Stevens Publishing, 2019. | Series: Ultimate science lab | Includes glossary and index.
Identifiers: ISBN 9781538235300 (pbk.) | ISBN 9781538235324 (library bound) | ISBN 9781538235317 (6pack)
Subjects: LCSH: Sound--Experiments--Juvenile literature. | Sound--Juvenile literature.
Classification: LCC QC225.5 C5725 2019 | DDC 534.078--dc23

First Edition

Published in 2019 by
Gareth Stevens Publishing
111 East 14th Street, Suite 349
New York, NY 10003

Copyright © Arcturus Holdings Ltd, 2019

Author: Anna Claybourne
Science consultant: Thomas Canavan
Experiment illustrations: Jessica Secheret
Other illustrations: Richard Watson
Photos: Shutterstock
Design: Supriya Sahai, with Emma Randall
Editor: Joe Fullman, with Julia Adams

Printed in the United States of America

CPSIA compliance information: Batch #CW19GS: For further information contact Gareth Stevens, New York, New York at 1-800-542-2595.

CONTENTS

START EXPERIMENTING!

This book is packed with exciting experiments that go bang, shake and vibrate, or are so incredible you won't believe your eyes! But there's nothing magical in these pages—it's all real-life amazing SCIENCE.

BE ECO-FRIENDLY!

First things first. As scientists, we aim to be as environmentally friendly as possible. Experiments require lots of different materials, including plastic ones, so we need to make sure we reuse and recycle as much as we can ...

* Some experiments use plastic straws; rather than buying a large amount, ask in coffee shops or restaurants whether they can spare a few for your experiments.

* Old cereal boxes are great for experiments that use cardboard.

* Save old school worksheets and other paper you no longer need, to reuse for experiments.

WHAT YOU'LL NEED

You can do most of these experiments with everyday items you'll find around the house.

Some useful things to have handy are ...

* Paper and cardboard
* Pens and pencils
* String
* Glue
* Tape
* Straws (plastic ones are best)
* Plates, bowls, jugs, and plastic food containers
* Scissors
* Rubber bands
* Paper cups
* Balloons

STAY SAFE!

Experiments are fun, but some of them can be dangerous if they're not done carefully ... so don't forget these safety tips:

✴ You will need an adult to help with experiments that involve cooking and heating, matches and candles, and sharp cutting tools. Wherever an experiment has something like this in it, you'll see this sign to remind you:

⚠ ASK AN ADULT!

✴ Follow all the instructions carefully to make sure you use all the equipment and materials in a safe way.

✴ If an experiment requires you to stand on a chair, make sure you have someone to assist you. Check that the chair is placed in a stable position and ask the person helping you to hold the chair while you are using it.

✸ Stand back from anything that's moving fast, or that involves eruptions or explosions. And don't throw, shoot, or whirl things around unless you're completely sure there's no one nearby.

And remember...

Always do experiments somewhere that's easy to clean up, like a kitchen or bathroom—NOT on the fancy carpet! And make sure you do clean up after yourself. Some of these experiments are messy!

So, are you ready to see some science? Step this way ...

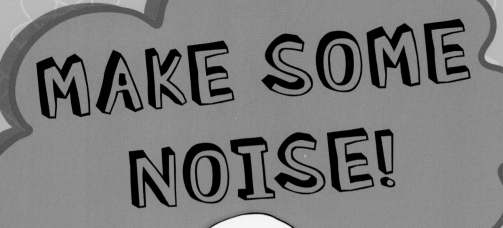

MAKE SOME NOISE!

The experiments in this book make loud bangs, weird noises, or cool music, to help you find out what sound really is and how it works.

What is sound?
Basically, we hear sound when things move and vibrate, or shake quickly to and fro. These movements make the air vibrate, too. The vibrations spread out through the air and reach our ears.

Sound waves
When you drop an object into liquid, it makes the water move, and ripples spread out in a circle until they touch the edge. Sound is the same, but instead of spreading out in a flat layer, the sound waves go in all directions.

Moving and shaking

For example, if someone hits a cymbal, the metal vibrates, and that makes invisible ripples, or sound waves, spread out in the air all around it. You hear the sound when the sound waves reach your ears.

Make a noise!

There are lots of ways to make a sound by getting something to vibrate. Try this simple experiment with a balloon:

1. Blow up a balloon, but don't tie it closed.

2. Hold the sides of the opening of the balloon, and pull them away from each other.

3. Slowly let the air out of the balloon. Try stretching the opening tightly and less tightly as the air escapes to see if you can change the sound.

Watch it

Sound vibrations are often so small or so fast that they can be hard to see clearly. But in this case, you should be able to see the neck of the balloon vibrating in a blur.

HOW DOES IT WORK?

As the air pushes through the narrow gap in the opening, it makes the rubbery balloon skin vibrate. This makes a loud squeaking sound.

GLITTER DISCO

This experiment will let you see the vibrations that sounds make—and get some glitter to dance!

WHAT YOU'LL NEED:

* A large radio with a speaker on the front, or a hi-fi speaker
* Glitter flakes (not the powdery kind—larger flakes work better)
* A large plastic plate or round tray
* Plastic wrap

1. Tear off a large piece of plastic wrap and stretch it over the plate so that it's as flat and smooth as possible. Tuck the plastic wrap under the plate to hold it in place.

2. Get your radio or speaker, and lie it down so that the speaker part is facing upward. You may have to ask someone to hold it steady.

3. Put your plastic wrap-covered plate right over the middle of the speaker. If you can see two speaker openings, use the bigger one if there is one.

4. Shake a small amount of glitter onto the middle of the plastic wrap—about a teaspoonful. (Be careful not to spill glitter into the speaker.)

5. Play some music—something with a clear beat, like rock, disco, or dance music—and turn it up loud (or as loud as you're allowed!).

HOW DOES IT WORK?
When the speaker makes sound, the sound makes vibrations in the air. They pass through the plate into the plastic wrap, making it vibrate up and down. Louder sounds make bigger vibrations! This makes the glitter jump in the air and move in time to the music.

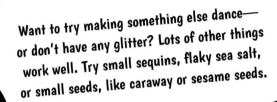

Want to try making something else dance—or don't have any glitter? Lots of other things work well. Try small sequins, flaky sea salt, or small seeds, like caraway or sesame seeds.

STRAW TROMBONE

If you have a real trombone and know how to play it, you'll definitely be able to make a racket. But if not, here's the next best thing—a working trombone made out of household items!

WHAT YOU'LL NEED:

* ✹ Two straws, one slightly wider than the other
* ✹ A piece of thin cardboard at least 6 x 6 inches (15 x 15 cm)
* ✹ A pencil
* ✹ Scissors
* ✹ Clear tape

From the side, your straw should look like this.

1. Take the narrower straw, and flatten one end of it between your fingers. Then use the scissors to carefully snip off the sides to form a point.

2. Press the end again until it's as flat as you can make it. Then test it to see if it makes a sound. Put the cut end of the straw about 1 inch (2.5 cm) inside your mouth, and blow hard. If there's no sound, press the end flat again.

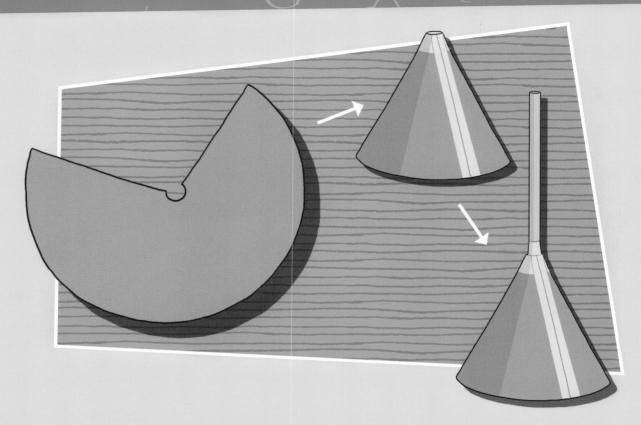

3. Copy this shape onto the cardboard, making it about 6 inches (15 cm) across, and cut it out. Curve it into a cone, with a straw-sized hole at the top, and tape in place. Stick one end of the wider straw into the cone, and tape together.

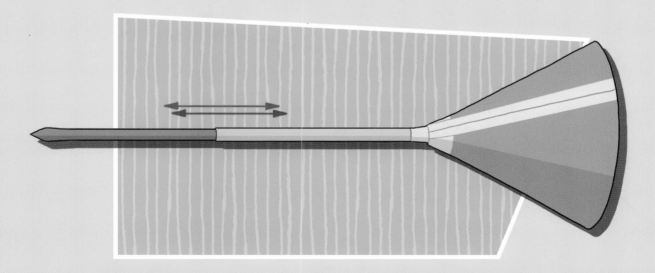

4. Now slide the wider straw over the narrower straw, so that it can slide up and down. Your trombone is ready to play!

HOW DOES IT WORK?

When you blow into the straw, your breath makes the pieces at the cut end vibrate, and this makes a noise. The air inside the straws vibrates, too. The longer the tube, the more space the air has to vibrate, and the lower the sound will be. The cone, or "bell," on the end of the trombone helps to make the sound louder.

Can you use the sliding movement to make higher and lower notes? This will work best if the straws are only slightly different sizes and fit together tightly.

SCI-FI SOUNDS

With nothing more than a metal spring toy and a paper cup, you can make a sound like a sci-fi spaceship zapping an alien enemy with a laser gun. Try it and see!

WHAT YOU'LL NEED:

* ✹ A metal spring toy, the type that "walks" down stairs
* ✹ A paper cup
* ✹ Clear tape
* ✹ Pointy scissors or a craft knife
* ✹ A metal spoon or fork
* ⓘ ASK AN ADULT!

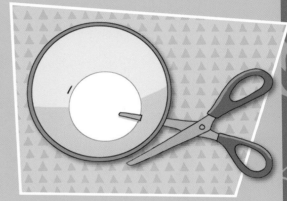

1. Ask an adult to cut two small, horizontal slots near the bottom of the cup, using the scissors or knife. They should be right next to the base of the cup, just above it.

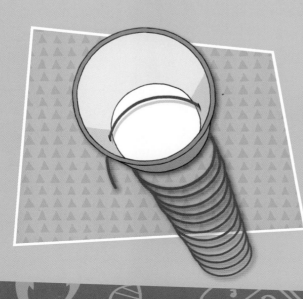

2. Now take the end of the spring toy and carefully slide it through both the slots, so that the first part of the spring lies flat against the cup base.

3. Hold the cup up in the air, so that the spring toy dangles down, almost touching the floor. (You might need to stand on a chair for this.)

HOW DOES IT WORK?

The space-age sound is created by lots of vibrations moving up the spring from the ground. The faster vibrations make higher-pitched sounds, which reach the cup first, followed by the lower ones. This makes the metallic "Pneeeeow!" noise that sounds like a space weapon.

To make the sound louder, tape a piece of cardboard around the cup in a cone shape to act as a megaphone.

4. To make the ray gun effect, make the spring toy bounce off the floor. The sound will come out of the cup. You can also try hitting the spring with the spoon.

BOTTLE BAGPIPE

This bizarre instrument makes a noise a bit like a bagpipe—or maybe a buzzing fly, or a ship's foghorn. See what you think it sounds like!

WHAT YOU'LL NEED:
* A small or medium-sized drink bottle made of tough plastic
* A balloon
* Pointy scissors
* A straw
* Clear tape
* Paper

(!) **ASK AN ADULT!**

1.
Ask an adult to cut the top off the bottle as neatly as possible. Then ask them to make a small hole in the side of the bottle, the same size as the straw, by sticking the pointy tip of the scissors into the plastic and twisting it around.

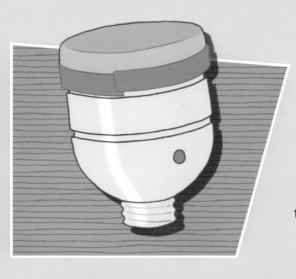

2.
Next, cut the open end off the balloon and stretch it as tightly as you can over the open end of the bottle. When it's as tight and flat as you can get it, fix the edge to the bottle with sticky tape.

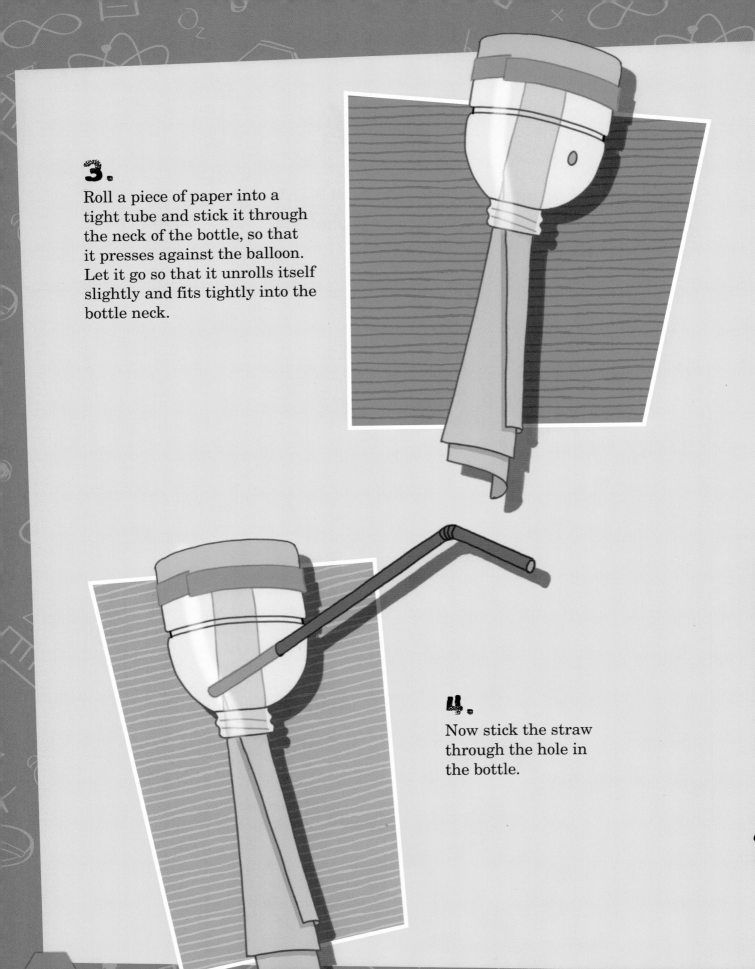

3.

Roll a piece of paper into a tight tube and stick it through the neck of the bottle, so that it presses against the balloon. Let it go so that it unrolls itself slightly and fits tightly into the bottle neck.

4.

Now stick the straw through the hole in the bottle.

5.

Hold the bottle in one hand and the paper tube in the other. Pushing the paper tube gently against the balloon, blow hard into the straw.

HOW DOES IT WORK?

When you blow air into the bottle, it pushes against the balloon and makes it vibrate. The vibrations spread into the paper tube, too, making a noise that comes out of the end of the tube.

SMARTPHONE SPEAKERS

These fantastic speakers will turn the tinny sound of a smartphone into a homemade boombox. All you need are some paper cups and a paper towel tube.

WHAT YOU'LL NEED:

* ✹ The tube from the inside of a paper towel roll
* ✹ 2 paper cups
* ✹ A pencil
* ✹ Pointy scissors
* ✹ A smartphone with music stored on it

⚠ ASK AN ADULT!

If you don't have a paper towel tube, you can use part of a poster tube, or the cardboard tube from inside a roll of wrapping paper. Ask an adult to cut it to about 10 inches (25 cm) long.

1. Hold the end of the tube against the side of one of the cups, close to the bottom. Draw around the tube with the pencil to make a circle.

2. Cut out the circle, with an adult's help, cutting very slightly inside the line you have drawn. Then do the same thing with the other cup.

3. Hold the end of your smartphone against the middle of the tube, and draw around it with the pencil. Ask an adult to help you cut out the shape, cutting just inside the line.

4. Now push the ends of the tube into the holes in the paper cups, as far as they will go.

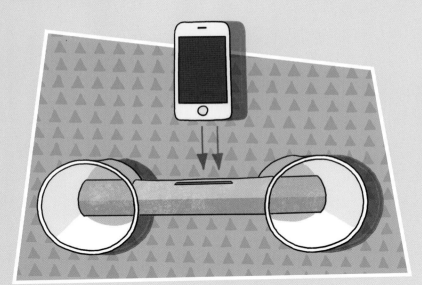

5. Stand the speakers on a table. Start some music playing on the phone, and push it into the hole in the tube.

HOW DOES IT WORK?
When the smartphone plays music, the vibrations spread out in all directions, so they don't sound very loud. When the phone is in the speakers, the vibrations spread into the tube, and then into the paper cups and the air inside them. This collects the sound and makes it point in one direction, so it sounds louder.

WHIRLING WHIRRER

Whirl this around your head and it will make a weird whirring sound. The secret is in the rubber band—make sure you use a really wide one!

WHAT YOU'LL NEED:

* ✸ A 6-inch (15 cm) ruler
* ✸ A short but thick rubber band, about ½ inch (1 cm) wide
* ✸ A piece of string about 3 feet (1 m) long
* ✸ A postcard
* ✸ Craft foam
* ✸ Scissors
* ✸ Clear tape

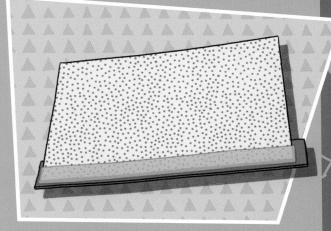

1. First, tape one edge of the postcard to the ruler, so that it sticks out slightly to one side, like this.

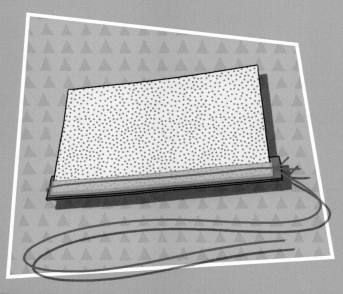

2. Tie one end of the string lengthwise around the ruler, and tape it in place, too.

3. Cut two pieces of craft foam, each about ½ x 2 inches (1 x 5 cm). Fold them around the ends of the ruler, letting the long end of the string hang free.

What could possibly go wrong? You could whack someone on the head or knock everything off a shelf, that's what! So make sure you ONLY do this in a large room with no one else in the way.

4. Stretch the rubber band around the ruler and over the pieces of foam.

5. Now hold the other end of the string, find a nice big empty space, and whirl the whirrer fast around your head.

HOW DOES IT WORK?

As the whirrer flies around, the air pushes against the rubber band and makes it vibrate, making a noise. When the whirrer moves faster, the rubber band vibrates faster, which makes a higher-pitched sound. The postcard helps to keep the whirrer flat as it flies. The air rushing past it pushes the postcard from above and below, making the whirrer stay level.

WHY DO BALLOONS POP?

Balloons are fun, but sooner or later they POP! What makes that loud popping noise, and why? Banish nervous people to a different room for this loud experiment!

WHAT YOU'LL NEED:
* ★ Several balloons
* ★ A candle and candleholder
* ★ Matches
* ★ Paper
* ★ Scissors
* ★ A pin for popping!

! ASK AN ADULT!

1.
Blow up your balloons and tie them closed. Keep them in a safe place away from your experiment area.

2.
Cut some little figures out of your paper, with rectangles at the bottom, like this. Fold the rectangles flat so your figures will stand up.

3.

Hold a balloon about 6 inches (15 cm) away from your paper figures, and pop the balloon with a pin. What happens to the people?

4.

Ask an adult to put your candle in its holder and light it with a match. Again, hold a balloon 6 inches (15 cm) away and pop it with a pin. What happens to the candle?

HOW DOES IT WORK?

When you blow up a balloon, you fill it with lots of air. The air is under a lot of pressure—it's tightly squashed inside the balloon. When you pop a balloon, the squashed air suddenly escapes. It rushes outward at high speed. This makes a strong ripple in the air, called a pressure wave. It hits your ears as a loud bang and can also blow out a candle or blow over a paper figure.

Explosions cause a pressure wave, too. That's why when there's an explosion, the things around it can get blown apart or blown away.

HOW FAST IS SOUND?

By now you know that when something makes a sound, sound waves travel through the air from where the sound started to your ears. In this experiment, you can see how long this takes.

WHAT YOU'LL NEED:
* At least two people
* A really big, wide-open space, like a playing field, sandy beach, or large playground
* 2 pan lids

800 feet (250 m)

1. One person should take both the pan lids and move really far away from the other person—ideally 800 feet (250 m) away or more. But they should still be able to see each other.

2. The first person should bang the pan lids together once, loudly. When the second person *sees* the lids bang together, they should stick one hand in the air.

Bang!

HOW DOES IT WORK?

When the first person bangs the pan lids, the other person sees it pretty much right away because the speed of light is so incredibly fast. However, the speed of sound is much slower. This means that the sound of the bang takes a while to catch up as the sound spreads out through the air.

3. Then, when the second person *hears* the sound of the lids banging together, they should stick their other hand up.

4.

If you have someone else to help, too, they could use a timer or stopwatch to try to measure the difference between seeing and hearing the bang.

If you want, try some math, too. Measure the distance between the two people and the time the sound takes to travel. With these (and maybe an adult to help), can you work out a figure for the speed of sound? It may be easier to calculate the figure using metric measurements, so it might look something like this:

Distance: 300 m
Sound travel time: about 1 second
Speed: 300 m per second
Speed in km per hour: ?
SPEED IN MILES PER HOUR: ?

29

GLOSSARY

bagpipe A musical instrument that is made up of a bag with reed pipes attached. The bag is filled with air and squeezed, pushing the air through the reed pipes. Bagpipes are traditionally played in countries such as Scotland and Ireland.

banish To send someone away.

boombox A large, portable stereo system that has a powerful sound.

foghorn A device that makes a deep, loud sound to warn ships in fog.

megaphone A funnel-shaped device that is used to make a voice sound louder.

metric Units of measurement based on the meter.

ripple One of a series of small waves.

sci-fi Short for "science fiction."

tinny Having a thin, metallic sound.

vibrate To shake very quickly.

zap To destroy.

FURTHER INFORMATION

Books

Andrews, Georgina, and Kate Knighton. *100 Science Experiments*. London, UK: Usborne Publishing, 2012.

DK Publishing. *101 Great Science Experiments*. London, UK: DK Publishing, 2015.

Isaac, Dawn. *101 Brilliant Things For Kids To Do With Science*. London, UK: Kyle Books, 2017.

Shaha, Alom and Emily Robertson. *Mr Shaha's Recipes for Wonder: Adventures in Science Round the Kitchen Table*. London, UK: Scribe UK, 2018.

Usborne Publishing. *365 Science Activities*. London, UK: Usborne Publishing, 2014.

Websites

http://www.sciencekids.co.nz/experiments.html
A whole host of experiments that let you explore the world of science.

https://www.youtube.com/watch?v=aAMW_3kWUhE
This video will show you how to make a screaming balloon!

https://www.exploratorium.edu/snacks/subject/sound
Discover over 25 science experiments that explore sound.

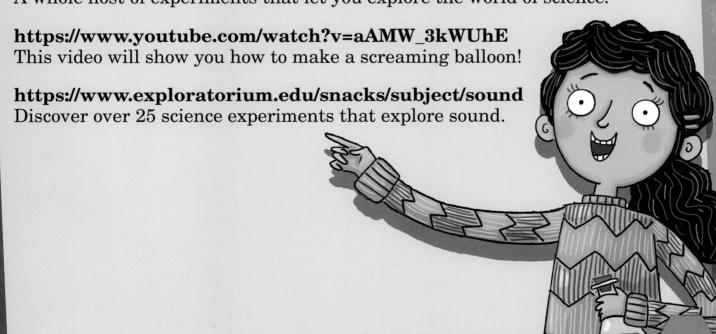

INDEX